Magic Glasses Day

By Alan Trussell-Cullen

Illustrated by Rae Dale

Chapter 1

Brad in Trouble – Again!

Brad always seemed to be in trouble.

Miss Hopkins, his teacher, was always saying things like: Stop talking, Brad!
Stop fidgeting, Brad!
Do your work, please, Brad!

One day Miss Hopkins asked the children to say what they liked best about school.

Some said it was reading stories. Some said it was writing stories. Some said it was doing math. Some said it was drawing pictures.

"What about you, Brad?" said Miss Hopkins. "What do you like best about school?"

Brad thought for a moment. "Eating my lunch," he replied.

The other children laughed, but Miss Hopkins looked upset.

When the children went out to play, Miss Hopkins asked Brad to stay behind. "There must be other things you like about school," she said. "What about reading?"

Brad shook his head.

"Why don't you like reading?" said Miss Hopkins.

"I like it when *you* read stories to *us*," said Brad, "but when I look at a book, the words go all funny."

"What about math?" said Miss Hopkins.

"Same thing," said Brad. "The numbers sort of shake like jelly, and I can't see them."

"What about writing stories?" said Miss Hopkins.

"I like *telling* stories," said Brad, "but when I try to write them down, the words go all fuzzy."

Chapter 2

Brad's Big Secret

Brad's teacher asked his mom and dad to come and see her. "Has Brad ever had his eyesight tested?" she asked.

"Oh, yes," said Brad's mom. "He has his eyes tested every year to make sure his glasses are right for him."

Miss Hopkins looked surprised. "Brad has glasses?" she asked.

"Oh, yes," said Brad's father.

"That's funny," said Miss Hopkins. "He never wears them at school."

Miss Hopkins opened Brad's desk. Sure enough, way at the back, tucked under all his books and papers, she found a glasses case.

"It looks like he's been trying to hide them," said Miss Hopkins.

"Perhaps he doesn't like wearing glasses in front of the other children," said Brad's mom.

"He doesn't like being different," said his dad.

"What should we do?" asked Brad's mom.

Miss Hopkins smiled. "Leave it to me," she said.

Chapter 3

Magic Glasses Day

The next Friday, Brad was home from school with a bad cold.

That day Miss Hopkins read the children a story about magic glasses, and then she helped them all make their own magic glasses.

They cut them out of cardboard, painted them with bright colors, and stuck glitter all over them. Even Miss Hopkins made a pair for herself.

When they had finished, she told the children that next Monday was Magic Glasses Day, and everyone had to wear their magic glasses at school all day. The children laughed and thought this was a wonderful idea.

"Good morning, class," said Miss Hopkins on Monday. "I'm glad you all remembered that today is Magic Glasses Day."

Brad looked around the classroom, and sure enough everyone was wearing a pair of amazing glasses – everyone except him. He didn't like feeling different.

"Please, Miss Hopkins," he said. "I don't have any magic glasses."

Miss Hopkins smiled. "Take a look in your desk," she said.

Brad opened his desk. He couldn't see any magic glasses.

"They're in your magic glasses case," whispered Miss Hopkins.

Brad opened the case. There were his old glasses, but someone had stuck some cardboard over the frame and then painted it and put glitter all over it. He put them on and looked around at the other children.

"Wow, Brad!" the other children said. "You look really cool!"

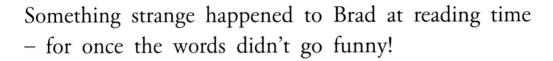

Chapter 4
A Big Surprise for Brad

Something strange happened to Brad at reading time – for once the words didn't go funny!

When they did math, he waited for the numbers to turn into jelly – but they didn't!

When he wrote his story, the words didn't go fuzzy. It was the best story he had ever written.

At the end of the day, Miss Hopkins took a photo of everyone wearing their magic glasses. The children all said how much they had enjoyed their Magic Glasses Day, especially Brad.

"My glasses really are magic!" said Brad. "I can see things properly."

His teacher smiled. "I think you should wear your magic glasses every day," she said.

"I will," said Brad. "Thanks, Miss Hopkins."

Then he ran off to catch up with his friends. They all walked home together wearing their magic glasses.